At
Her Majesty's
Request

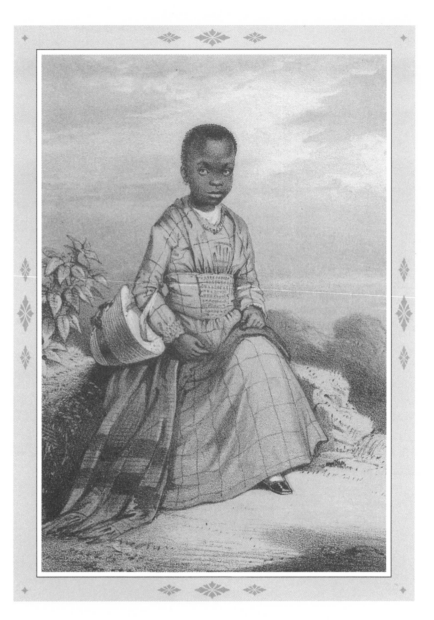

At Her Majesty's Request

AN AFRICAN PRINCESS IN VICTORIAN ENGLAND

by Walter Dean Myers

SCHOLASTIC PRESS   NEW YORK

LIBRARY OF CONGRESS CATALOGING-IN-PUBLICATION DATA

Myers, Walter Dean, 1937-

At her majesty's request: an African princess in Victorian England / by Walter Dean Myers.   p. cm.

Includes bibliographical references. Summary: Biography of the African princess saved from execution and taken to England, where Queen Victoria oversaw her upbringing and where she lived for a time before marrying an African missionary.   ISBN 0-590-48669-1   1. Bonetta, Sarah Forbes, b. 1843?—Juvenile literature. 2. Victoria, Queen of Great Britain, 1819-1901—Friends and associates—Juvenile literature. 3. Great Britain—Court and courtiers—History—19th century—Juvenile literature. 4. Missionaries' spouses—Africa, West—Biography—Juvenile literature. 5. Africans—Great Britain—History—19th century—Juvenile literature. 6. Princesses—Nigeria—Oyo State—Biography—Juvenile literature. 7. Nigerians—Great Britain—Biography—Juvenile literature. [1. Bonetta, Sarah Forbes, b. 1843? 2. Victoria, Queen of Great Britain, 1819-1901—Friends and associates. 3. Great Britain—Court and courtiers. 4. Princesses. 5. Women—Biography.] I. Title.

DA565.F67M94 1999   941.08′092—dc21   [B] 98-7217   CIP   AC

10   9   8   7   6   5   4   3   2   1   9/9   0/0   01   02   03

Printed in the U.S.A.   37

FIRST EDITION, FEBRUARY 1999

The text type was set in 12.5-point Monotype Scotch Roman.

Book design by David Saylor

For

Autumn, Beverly,

Bianca, and Summer,

the princesses in my life

TABLE OF CONTENTS

Introduction

I'VE ALWAYS found old bookstores exciting. Whenever I'm in a city that's new to me, I immediately look through the telephone directory for BOOKS, USED AND RARE. Book dealers send me their catalogs, and I read them as carefully as I would a letter from an old friend, never knowing what treasure I might find. Sometimes the catalogs contain printed material other than books, such as old photographs, newspapers, pamphlets, postcards, and letters. Such was the case of a catalog I received from a small book-and-ephemera shop in London.

One of the items for sale was a group of letters concerning a young girl who had lived in England in the mid-nineteenth century. The brief description of the material was intriguing. The girl, supposedly an African princess, had been rescued from a certain and horrible death in Africa. According to the catalog, she had been brought to England, and Queen Victoria had later been the godmother of her first child. The story sounded fascinating, but I had been on wild-goose chases before, and I approached the material with caution. I had a trip to London planned for the fall and put off thinking about the letters until then.

London in November. The weather was crisp but not overly cold and the streets bustled with early Christmas shoppers. I phoned the shop to ask if the letters were still available. They were, I was told. I could see them if I stopped by the following afternoon. When I arrived the next day, I was handed a folder with about fifty letters and some sheets of printed material. A few of the letters were scarcely readable. Others were fairly clear but cross-written; that is, the writer had written a message, then turned the paper sidewise and written over the first message. An accompanying article had a poor copy of a photograph of Sarah Forbes Bonetta, which was the English name of the young princess.

The price the dealer was asking for the letters was not terribly high, but I still wondered if there were really a story to be found in the papers before me. I decided to find out.

Back home I began the hard job of piecing together Sarah's life. Much to my surprise, I found I already owned an account of her rescue in a book called *Dahomey and the Dahomans*, written by the man who had saved Sarah from death, Frederick E. Forbes. In the book there is a delicate drawing of a young black girl. I realized that somewhere between the Victorian dress she wore and the African tribal scars etched into her face was the girl I wanted to write about.

I hired an English researcher who knew about the school Sarah had attended. A photography dealer at a flea market in New York told me about the Royal Archives at Windsor Castle. A letter to the castle produced two photographs. One was of Sarah, taken in 1856. The other, undated, was of her daughter Victoria. I also received fascinating excerpts from Queen Victoria's diary.

Slowly, the story of Sarah Forbes Bonetta began to emerge. Here was the tale of an African princess under the protection of Queen Victoria, one of the most powerful people in the world. Here was a young woman struggling for independence in Victorian England. Most of all, here was a dynamic soul who lived and loved through one of the most exciting times in history.

I am deeply moved by Sarah's life and struggles. There is joy here, and sorrow. There is the triumph of the human spirit and more than a touch of tragedy. Here, to the best of my ability, is her story.

At
Her Majesty's
Request

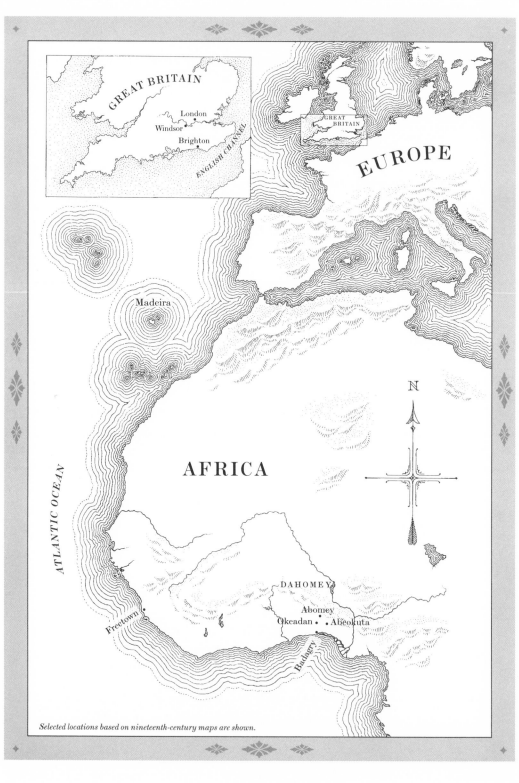

GREAT BRITAIN

London

Windsor

Brighton

ENGLISH CHANNEL

GREAT BRITAIN

EUROPE

Madeira

AFRICA

ATLANTIC OCEAN

N

DAHOMEY

Abomey

Okeadan · Abeokuta

Freetown

Badagry

Selected locations based on nineteenth-century maps are shown.

1848

The Capture

THE ATTACK came in the middle of the night. The Egbado village of Okeadan was surrounded by Dahomian raiders. First, houses on the edge of the village were set on fire. As the flames danced crazily in the air, the sounds of fiercely pounded drums and the high-pitched voices of Dahomian women warriors filled the night. The men of the village rushed from their homes and tried to form a circle of defense.

The Dahomans fired their long rifles into the defensive circle. Overwhelmed, the Egbadoes tried to surrender. Hundreds were slaughtered without mercy; only the youngest and strongest, those most likely to be bought in the slave markets, were spared. The houses of the chiefs and royal families were in the middle of the village, and these were furiously attacked. A family was dragged out from one of these homes and the father and mother forced to their knees. Swords were lifted, catching the glint of the flames that burned the village. The swords were crashed down on the necks of the village chief and his wife. Their children, one a five-year-old girl, looked on with horror.

The entire village was brutally destroyed. The houses were burned, the storehouses looted and torn down. Everyone not killed was rounded up and bound as the Dahomans fired over their heads. The captives, under the constant taunts of the Dahomans, were then marched through the night. Most were being taken to Whydah, where thousands of Africans before them had been sold into slavery. A few were selected to be taken to Abomey, the capital of Dahomey. There they would be saved, only to be sacrificed in bloody Dahomian rituals. Such was the power and ruthlessness of the king of Dahomey, a man known throughout West Africa as Gezo.

But there were other strong men in West Africa. One of them, the young British captain of the HMS *Bonetta*, was as much against the slave trade and the slaughter of innocent people as King Gezo was indifferent to it.

The HMS *Bonetta* dropped anchor off the coast of Africa in October of 1849. Thirty-year-old Commander Frederick Forbes's mission was to help in stopping the slave trade. The Dahomans played a major role in that trade. The very mention of King Gezo's name was enough to upset a village, such was his reputation for ferocity and cruelty. Forbes knew his task would not be easy. Europeans who went even briefly into the African interior did so at great risk to their health. Tropical diseases took the lives of many who ventured there. Further, the slave trade had broken down much of the order of West African society, and the men who set themselves up as kings and chiefs considered all outsiders a

GEZO, KING OF DAHOMEY

threat to their influence. The terror of the slave trade and the raids all contributed to Gezo's power.

If Commander Forbes had any doubts about the reputation of the Dahomans, he lost them as he approached King Gezo's palace in early June 1850.

> The walls of the palace of Dange-lah-cordeh are surmounted, at a distance of twenty feet, with human skulls, many of which ghastly ornaments time has decayed, and the wind blown down.
>
> —*DAHOMEY AND THE DAHOMANS*

The Dahomans wanted all of West Africa and the rest of the world to know about their ferocity. To King Gezo, the skulls lining the walls were a sign of his strength. The terror that the skulls represented were, in his mind, an indication of his enormous power.

There were many rituals to go through before King Gezo would allow Commander Forbes to meet him face-to-face. Commander Forbes followed them all dutifully. Ministers of King Gezo approached the small British expedition and exchanged greetings. Commander Forbes noticed that the number of his party was being counted in case there was to be a confrontation. The Dahomans gave Commander Forbes and his party gifts, and expected gifts in return, which they received. King Gezo knew that Commander Forbes represented the most powerful navy in the world and wanted his respect. The commander and his party were seated on a high platform facing a courtyard. Hundreds of African warriors, male and female, paraded in front of the British naval group, reciting the many accomplishments of their leader. This display of warriors and skulls was meant to impress the English officer, but it was also part of an important Dahomian ceremony. This day was the beginning of the ritual known in Dahomey as *Ek-onee-noo-ah-toh*. It would be a ceremony of human sacrifice.

Finally, King Gezo himself came to the platform, accompanied by his Amazon bodyguards. There were greetings and the introductions that Forbes knew he must engage in. But when the polite talk had ended, Forbes immediately brought up his displeasure with the slave trade. King Gezo listened patiently. Forbes represented a power equal to his own, King Gezo knew, and also a source of revenue.

"I am the first of the blacks," King Gezo said. "As your queen is the first of the whites. I do what I wish, as your queen does."

What Commander Forbes had to offer was a way of improving the economy of Dahomey without slavery. The key for Dahomey, the British naval officer said, was to increase the production of palm oil. If Dahomey abandoned the slave trade, the British would buy a great deal of palm oil to make up the money lost from the slave trade.

But for the Dahomans the slave trade meant more than just a way of keeping the economy going. The Europeans who wanted to buy human beings for labor had provided guns and European goods, which not only made the Dahomans rich but gave them crucial power over their enemies. If King Gezo gave up the terror he was inflicting on his fellow Africans to become a peaceful trader in palm oil, he would be far less powerful than the rulers of other kingdoms in the area.

King Gezo was very open in his refusal to give up the slave trade. There was profit in palm oil, he felt, but little power.

Commander Forbes was frustrated and angry. A member of the Royal Navy since he was fourteen, he had seen the misery that the slave trade caused. He had personally rescued many Africans who were headed for lives of bondage.

As Commander Forbes continued his talks with King Gezo, the rituals of the Dahomian holiday continued, too. The long Dane rifles the warriors carried were fired into the air. Drums were beaten. Warriors danced, swinging their weapons overhead. Forbes, a military man, began to count the actual number of warriors that King Gezo commanded. He suspected that the Dahomian king was trying to make the size and strength of his army seem greater by having his warriors circle several times in front of the British visitors.

Commander Forbes tried to conceal his dislike for King Gezo. He didn't comment as the warriors placed their tributes before their leader, or as they marched in review, waving their banners as Gezo sat under a wide umbrella.

Suddenly, a scream pierced the air, and the men in Forbes's party looked to where a group of Dahomans were waving their guns in delight. The festivities had suddenly taken a horrible turn. Through an interpreter, Commander Forbes learned that the people he saw being carried in small baskets were about to be put to death. The ceremony was called the "watering of the graves." The victims, dressed in simple white garments, were to be killed and their blood smeared on the graves of important Dahomans. It was the Dahomian way of honoring their ancestors. Some of the intended victims had been held for over two years for this critical moment. Bound hand and foot, they were being carried in small baskets above the heads of Dahomian soldiers. The Dahomans mocked the victims and prodded them with spears and knives as they were brought through the ranks.

Commander Forbes watched in horror as a man was

taken to a pit, the basket tipped and the man thrown down viciously. As his body hit the ground, he was instantly attacked and his head cut off.

Commander Forbes desperately tried to make King Gezo stop the slaughter. Gezo dismissed the British naval officer with a wave of his hand. Commander Forbes offered money. The King allowed his court officers to bargain for several of the victims. But the ritual of watering the graves of the ancestors was an old custom, King Gezo's interpreters explained, and it could not be stopped without bringing dishonor to the people of Dahomey.

Commander Forbes had never seen such a cruel and bloody ritual. In all his years of fighting the slave trade, he was sure that this was the worst moment he had ever experienced. Then he saw the girl.

She was so small, so still. The drums beat louder as they brought her toward the pit. The warrior carried her with ease over his shoulders.

Commander Forbes was horrified. He couldn't believe that a king could kill a child in a ritual. But Gezo had no

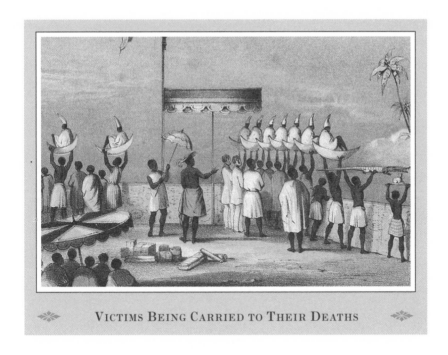

problem at all in sacrificing the girl. She was an Egbado, it was explained, an enemy of the Dahomans. The tribal markings on her face showed that she was of royal blood. Her blood on the graves of the King's ancestors would be an honor to them.

There were other reasons for King Gezo's parade of soldiers and for the brutality that he openly displayed to Commander Forbes. The British in Africa always negoti-

THE WATERING OF THE GRAVES

ated from a position of strength. They would make
peaceful treaties when it served their interests, but would
not hesitate to use force when they felt it was the best
method of achieving their ends. Earlier, in April of 1847,
King Gezo had made a treaty of friendship and com-
merce with Britain, but the British negotiations for
ending the slave trade had not been successful. Gezo
knew that a British force, including Forbes's ship, had

attacked and destroyed the slave pens at Gallinas in February 1849, just a few months earlier. The British Foreign Secretary, Lord Palmerston, made it clear in a letter to John Beecroft, the British consul to Africa, that military action was possible against Gezo.

25 FEBRUARY 1850

With respect to any aggressive intentions of the King of Dahomey towards the Yoruba people, you will have an opportunity, during your visit to Abomey, to bring that subject under the notice of the king; you will represent to him that the people who dwell in the Yoruba and Popo Countries are the friends of England....Moreover, there are dwelling among those tribes liberated Africans and British-born subjects whom Her Majesty's Government are bound to protect from injury....

Gezo felt the need to display his own power to the British group.

Commander Forbes continued to protest the killing of

the girl, but the small band of British sailors could not force King Gezo's soldiers to stop. Forbes himself was in Africa to end the slave trade, not to wage war against the Dahomans.

Commander Forbes challenged King Gezo. Queen Victoria would never kill an innocent child and would not respect him if he did so.

For the first time King Gezo hesitated. It was important for him to be respected as a great leader. He spoke to his ministers. The girl had been kept alive in captivity for two years. The King could not stop a practice that his people had carried out for so many years. But he also understood that it was not wise to anger the powerful British. When the conference with his ministers ended, it was announced that the killing of the adults would continue. The girl, however, would be given to Commander Forbes's queen. She would be a present from the King of the blacks to the Queen of the whites.

The girl was shaking in terror when she was brought before Commander Forbes. She had seen many of her people killed in these rituals and knew that her time had come. Her eyes were wide as she looked at Commander Forbes. She still wore the white garment that had been put on her in preparation for her death.

When he learned that she spoke Yoruba, he told her through an interpreter that she would not be harmed. But King Gezo had also told the girl that she would not be harmed.

Commander Forbes lifted her chin gently and examined the tribal marks on her cheeks. Those marks, lines cut into her face as an infant showing that she was a princess, had saved her from a life of slavery but had brought her to this dreadful place. Commander Forbes tried to let her know that she was now safe, but he could not erase the fear from her eyes. Later, when he left the palace, the girl was with him.

Abomey, the capital of Dahomey, was fifty-seven miles through rough country to the sea where the *Bonetta* was anchored. After their journey Commander Forbes took the girl aboard the ship and sailed down the coast to Badagry, in what is now Nigeria. The Church Missionary Society, an organization of missionaries from the Church

of England, had a station there, and he brought the girl to them. The society had been in West Africa for many years, bringing their religious teachings to the native population.

The girl remembered little from the raid at Okeadan in which she had been captured. She knew her parents had been killed. She had no idea what had happened to her brothers and sisters. Much of what she had experienced had been so horrible that she had simply shut it out of her mind. Forbes's heart went out to her. When members of the Church Missionary Society asked what he would do with her, he said he would take her to England. Officially, she had been given to the Queen. It was decided that she should be baptized, and this was arranged at the mission church at Badagry. When asked what name she should receive, Commander Forbes gave her the name of Sarah Forbes Bonetta.

The missionaries at Badagry dressed Sarah in English clothes. The wife of the Reverend Vidal painted a watercolor portrait of her.

By now, the *Bonetta*'s tour of duty was over and it was

time to return to England. A warship, the *Bonetta* was not designed to accommodate a little girl, but the sailors fixed a place for her and spent much of their free time amusing her.

The white sailors seemed friendly enough and Sarah — or Sally, as they began to call her — grew less afraid. She was still dressed in clothes provided by the missionaries. She had never seen dresses such as the English wore or eaten the kinds of food she was now being given. The sailors started teaching her English and were delighted with how quickly she was able to learn the new language. Still, she stayed as close to Commander Forbes as she could. The young commander seemed glad to have her around him and spent as much time as he could with her. Somehow, through all of the horrible things that had happened to her, she still maintained a quiet strength. Sometimes Commander Forbes would hear her softly singing to herself. He wondered if the songs were ones she had learned among her own people or ones she had composed herself.

The *Bonetta*'s crew set a course for England. The ship

had already been away from England for nearly two years before Commander Forbes's meeting with King Gezo, and now it was time to head for home. The men were relieved to be away from the hardships of the African patrol and eager to see their families.

Commander Forbes didn't know what he was going to do with the girl once they returned to England. He thought about adopting her himself. He and his wife, Mary, already had four children of their own, but he felt that the young black girl would fit in nicely with the Forbes family.

1850

England for the First Time

THE DOCKS at Gravesend bustled with life as the *Bonetta* arrived at port in late July 1850. The guard was assigned, the ship secured, and men not on duty were released to visit their families. Commander Forbes took Sarah home with him to Winkfield Place, not far from Windsor Castle.

Commander Forbes wrote a detailed report of his mission to Africa. In the report he told of his meeting with **King Gezo** and the king's offer of the girl to Queen Victoria, as if the right to give one human being to another were so easily assumed. Slavery had been outlawed throughout the British Empire, and

QUEEN VICTORIA

Sarah would surely not belong to anyone.

Commander Forbes did not even consider the idea that the Queen of England would take notice of the little girl he had brought from Africa. But although Forbes despised King Gezo, he was still an African king who had given a present to Queen Victoria. Commander Forbes wrote a letter to his superiors about Sarah.

AUG. 3RD, 1850

The Secretary
of the Admiralty,

As a Government Officer I feel myself in duty bound to request their Lordships to lay the offer before Her Majesty, if they should approve thereof.

She now passes by the name of "Sarah Bonetta" and is an intelligent, good tempered (I need hardly add Black) girl, about six or seven years of age.

I have the honor to be

Sir

Your obedient servant

F. E. FORBES, LIEUTENANT COMMANDER

Commander Forbes had no idea what a difference that letter would make in young Sarah's life.

~

9 NOVEMBER 1850

WINDSOR CASTLE

When we came home, found Albert still here waiting for Capt. Forbes & a poor little Negro girl, whom he brought back from the King of Dahome, her parents & all her relations having been sacrificed. Capt. Forbes saved her life by asking for her as a present. She was brought into the Corridor. She is 7 years old, sharp & intelligent, & speaks English. She was dressed as any other girl. When her bonnet was taken off, her little black woolly head & big earrings gave her the true Negro type.

— FROM QUEEN VICTORIA'S DIARY

Queen Victoria, baptized Alexandrina Victoria, was born on the twenty-fourth of May, 1819. Her father, Edward, Duke of Kent, died when Victoria was still an infant, leaving her and her mother, also named Victoria, very much in debt and dependent on the goodwill of relatives. Her mother, the Duchess of Kent, kept young Victoria close to her at all times, away from other children her age. But while the girl was physically close to her mother, they were not emotionally close. The child spent many lonely hours with her dolls, pretending they were friends and making up lives that they would lead. Perhaps that is why she wanted to learn more about the young African girl who had lost both her parents.

When Victoria became Queen of England in 1837, she was unmarried. The eighteen-year-old met and fell in love with a handsome German prince named Albert, and they were soon wed. Victoria and the Prince Consort, as Albert was called, began their family at once. Their first child, Victoria, was born in 1840, then Albert Edward in 1841, Alice in 1843, Alfred in 1844, Helena in 1846, Louise in 1848, Arthur in 1850, and later, Leopold in 1853, and Beatrice in 1857.

By 1850, the young Queen Victoria was the most powerful monarch in the world. The average person in

ALBERT, THE PRINCE CONSORT

England had no hope of ever actually speaking to her, or of seeing her face-to-face. Visits to the palace were rare, even for foreign heads of state.

But the Queen commanded that Sarah be brought to

Windsor Castle, one of the royal residences, at eleven o'clock on Saturday, the ninth of November, 1850. The Queen's eldest son, Edward VII, was present, as was her daughter Victoria and other members of the royal family and household.

The Queen, who was impressed that Sarah had learned so much of the English language, listened as the child related as much of her story as she could.

After her capture, she had been brought before King Gezo, who had examined her face and the scars. He had told her that she would not be harmed, but the ones who fed her to keep her alive until her execution told her differently. She had been kept in a small space, and for weeks at a time did not see another person, just a bowl of food pushed through an opening in the wall. Occasionally, she was made to witness the other human victims being dragged out for sacrifice and knew that one day it would be her turn.

The Queen had heard from Commander Forbes how the young girl was known to be a princess by the tribal marks on her face. These tribal marks were an important part of Egbado identity. Even before it was officially time for Egbado children to receive the scars that told the world who they were, young Egbado girls put marks on their faces with dyes much as young English girls might powder theirs.

The Queen was very much interested in the relatively new art of photography. When the visit with Sarah had ended, the Queen had asked that Sarah have her picture taken. She was brought to the studio of John J. Mayall, an American photographer then working in England. Sarah did not know what the photographer intended and was fearful of him. Her fear grew to panic when she saw a portrait on the wall of a man wearing a sword.

"Cut head off!" she screamed, running her hand rapidly across her small throat. "Cut head off!"

Swords, Sarah had learned from her years in captivity, were for cutting off heads. The terrified girl, shaking with fright, had to be calmed and reassured that the man with the sword was not there and would not harm her.

Queen Victoria was deeply moved by Sarah's story. The Forbes family could indeed raise the child, but the Queen

SIR CHARLES BEAUMONT PHIPPS

would pay her expenses. She informed her personal secretary, C. B. Phipps, to make the necessary arrangements.

Sir Charles Beaumont Phipps was forty-nine years old. He was, officially, the Keeper of Her Majesty's Purse. His wife, Margaret Anne Phipps, often supervised the day-to-day affairs in the various palaces as they related to the Queen. It was she who would oversee Sarah's care. The Phippses also had several children of their own, the oldest being fairly close in age to Sarah.

～∽

As rare as it was for people to call upon the Queen, she truly seemed to enjoy seeing Sarah, and several visits were arranged.

11 JANUARY 1851

WINDSOR CASTLE

After luncheon Sally Bonita, the little African
girl, came with Mrs. Phipps, & showed me some of
her work. This is the 4th time I have seen the poor
child, who is really an intelligent little thing....

— FROM QUEEN VICTORIA'S DIARY

Here the Queen refers to Sarah as "Sally." It was common at the time for English people to have both a formal name and then a name that was used as a term of affection between friends. Among the royal children, Victoria was "Vicky"; Albert Edward, who would later become King of England on his mother's death, was known as

"Bertie"; Alfred was "Affie"; and Helena was "Lenchen."

The Queen also refers to Sarah's "work," the lessons she was taking from Mrs. Forbes and the Forbes children. In England in the mid-nineteenth century, there was no public school system. Most education was private, and few people could afford it. The Forbes family was quite wealthy. The Forbes children went to private schools. Though Sarah did not attend school, the education she was receiving at the Forbes home was putting her far ahead of most English children.

Her new life must have been exhilarating and close to overwhelming for her. There was so much in England that she had never seen before. In London the streets were bustling with activity. Gentlemen in tall hats strode quickly down Regent Street. Elegantly dressed women sat in carriages that rattled down Oxford Street. Vendors sold steaming hot chestnuts on the sidewalks. Boys carried signs advertising tailors. Newspapers were sold on the corners.

There were other blacks in England in 1850, but the chance of Sarah seeing any of them at Windsor was rare.

There were Africans who came to London on ships and worked at the docks. There were also black students, servants, and laborers, who mostly lived in the large cities. Occasional visitors from the United States, such as Frederick Douglass or William Wells Brown, men who had escaped slavery, came to England, too, usually for short periods of time. Sarah, who had lived among only black people for most of her life, now had to get used to living in a completely different world. Here there were little girls with blonde hair and blue eyes and what must have seemed to Sarah incredibly white skin.

Snow! What must she have thought of snow? To see all of London blanketed by soft, white flurries? To see the flakes on her bonnet when she came into the Forbes home and looked at herself in the mirror? But of all her experiences, nothing could have excited her as much as her visits to the palace and Queen Victoria. Sarah was taught to curtsy properly, and how to address the Queen. She learned to wear the clothes that Mrs. Forbes made and that friends of the family gave to her. But most of all she had to deal with the excitement of her status as a celebrity, a protégée of the Queen of England!

Any day that Sarah was scheduled to visit the Queen would start with an early-morning rise, washing, and family prayers. Breakfast would have been with the children, most likely brought to the table by a serving girl.

Then the clothes — which would have been selected days before — would be laid out and Sarah carefully dressed by Mrs. Forbes. The excitement would have grown with each passing moment. From the Forbes home they would have taken an early carriage ride to Windsor, with Commander Forbes reminding Sarah to be polite, to speak only when spoken to, and to try always to agree with the Queen.

Windsor Castle sits high on a hill. In winter, the wind can be bitterly cold as it whips through the turrets. The inclines leading to the castle are steep and treacherous when icy. But the inside of the castle is magnificent. Room after room is furnished with priceless treasures from around the world, representing all of the reaches of the British Empire. Paintings of the royal family by world-famous masters grace the walls.

THE WATERLOO CHAMBER, WINDSOR CASTLE

Before meeting the Queen, Sarah would have been given over to Mrs. Phipps, who would have inspected her to make sure that she was presentable to Her Majesty.

Queen Victoria was a small woman; at less than five feet she was not much taller than the children who were fortunate enough to be around her. When Sarah visited, the royal children would come to see her as well. Both Queen Victoria and Prince Albert were fond of having people from other lands at the palace. This interest was continued in their children. For Sarah, Princess Alice would be the most charming. The young Princess was Sarah's size, with a quick smile and a boldness that would have put Sarah at ease. It was with Princess Alice and the younger children that Sarah rode in the pony cart around the grounds of the palace.

Everything in England was new to Sarah. Everything in her life now was new to her. And, without a doubt, Sarah was new to the people of Windsor and London. While most of the English who lived in London had certainly seen black people, few had seen a young African girl who lived in such a manner as Sarah. Sarah

THE ROYAL PONY CART ON WHICH SARAH RODE

was always well dressed and accompanied wherever she went by someone of the wealthy Forbes family or someone from the palace. The story of her coming to England had been published in *Britannia* and other newspapers. She was not like the blacks that had come from America, or the entertainers, or the colorful black characters who scraped out their livings either begging or sweeping the streets. Sarah was a celebrity, a young girl of substance.

But living in England, living with a new family, living in a totally English culture, not to mention her visits to the Queen, meant that there was much that Sarah had to absorb. The upheaval was taxing on her. As the weather turned from the early winter months, chilly and dark and rainy in England, to the bleak coldness of mid-winter, Sarah began to come down with colds. She was taken to Dr. Brown, the Queen's doctor, who listened to her coughing and saw the stress she was under. Dr. Brown gave her medications but the coughing continued. As exciting as she found her new life, she didn't always have the strength to do all the things she wanted.

Most Africans had no difficulty adapting to cold weather. The slave trade had taken people of African ancestry to Great Britain, North and South America, and the Caribbean, and they had withstood the various climates with relative ease. Still, when Sarah did not respond quickly to treatment for her frequent illnesses, it was decided that perhaps the weather was too difficult for her. Would it be better for her, the Queen wondered, if she were back in Africa?

What happened to Sarah, and why it happened, can often only be a matter of guessing. Clues, however, present themselves when two or more documents or events are compared. Sarah is mentioned in the Queen's diary as having visited the palace on Saturday, the eleventh of January. Two weeks later a letter was sent from Charles Phipps to the Reverend Henry Venn, head of the Church Missionary Society in Africa.

The letter is an interesting one, as it is the first to describe Sarah as being formally under the Queen's protection.

WINDSOR CASTLE

JAN 25, 1851

The Queen has at present under her protection a little African girl, about 8 years old, who was brought to this Country by Commander Forbes from the King of Dahomey.

The Queen, having made enquiries, has been

informed that the climate of the Country is, often fatally, hurtful to the health of African children, and the Queen is therefore anxious that this child should be educated in one of Her Majesty's dependencies upon the Coast of Africa.

Though wrong, the idea that Sarah's health would be harmed in a colder climate was typical of medical thought in the nineteenth century. And when the Queen made up her mind, no one was going to oppose her.

Commander Forbes had already returned to sea, leaving Sarah with his wife and family. He was going back to Africa, more determined than ever to help put an end to the slave trade. Perhaps the blow of her having to leave England, where she was just beginning to feel comfortable, was softened by knowing that Commander Forbes, the man she identified most as her father, would also be in Africa.

Sarah had been strong enough to survive the raid on her village and the long journey to Dahomey. She had been strong enough to survive the months of captivity and the jarring transition to life in Britain. Now she would have to be strong enough to make the long journey back to Africa and to face an uncertain future in Sierra Leone.

Sierra Leone, a country in West Africa, had been established in the late eighteenth century as a place where Africans who had once been enslaved in England and the British colonies could rebuild their lives. Later, missionaries had built churches in Freetown, its capital, and other towns there in order to bring their Christian teachings to the area. Among the religious groups who had built missions in Sierra Leone was the Church Missionary Society. Commander Forbes had sought their help when he had first rescued Sarah, and now it was to one of their schools that Sarah was being sent by Queen Victoria.

Mrs. Forbes, who had taken to Sarah as much as her husband had, was heartbroken. She had really grown to love Sarah. But it was the Queen's will that the young girl return to Africa. The book that Commander Forbes had been writing about Dahomey was complete and off

THE CRYSTAL PALACE

to the publisher. Sarah knew her picture would be in it, as well as the story of her rescue. And Mrs. Forbes told her that they would never forget her and that, from time to time, she could return to England and stay with them as long as she wished. A flurry of activity ensued as Mary Forbes, with the help of the Queen and Mrs. Phipps, arranged to prepare a proper wardrobe for Sarah to take with her to Africa.

At this same time, all of London was excited about the opening of the Crystal Palace. Newspapers were full of pictures of the glass and iron structure that Prince Albert had directed. It was to house a grand exhibition of all the great technologies of the world. A sense of gaiety and accomplishment filled the air. But for Sarah, there was only more bad news. Commander Forbes had grown ill in Africa, and had died on the twenty-fifth of March.

Sarah was crushed. The young commander had saved her life, and she had hoped always to be near him. Now he was dead, buried at sea, and she would never see him again.

It was a tearful Sarah that arrived at the docks at Gravesend on the seventeenth of May, 1851. A Reverend Schmid was to accompany her back to Africa aboard the ship *Bathurst*. Reverend Schmid was a slight, intense man making his first trip to Africa. He was aware of the dangers he might encounter on that continent. His wife was with him, which gave him some comfort, but he was not at all sure of himself as he waited for the signal to board. He might have thought of the fact that a good many missionaries died within a year of arriving in Africa, usually from what they called the "fever." Sierra Leone, one writer explained, was the white man's grave. But Reverend Schmid had been entrusted by Mr. Phipps with the task of accompanying Sarah, and he had written a letter of thanks for the honor.

39 KINGSQUARE GOWELL-ROAD

MAY 16TH, 1851

Sir,

I have received your letter containing the list of Sally's articles, which were put on board the

Bathurst, *also the checque which you enclosed from Her Majesty. We will endeavor to do all what we can to take good care of Sally, whilst she is on board with us, as also for the articles she has and after our arrival in the Colony we hope the Lord will bless her education. With regard to the large present I can only say we acknowledge it as a token of Her Majesty's great kindness with humble gratitude; we have not deserved it, for taking care of Sally is but our duty. May the Lord bless the giver.*

We are very thankful to you, Sir, for your kind wishes. May the Lord Almighty realize them to us and to you.

Mrs. Schmid joins in kind regards to Mrs. Phipps and yourself.
Yours very sincerely,

D. M. SCHMID

There were many hugs and many tears as Sarah's luggage was loaded onto the ship. It had been in June of the previous year that Sarah had been saved from death by

Commander Forbes. In one short year she had been taken from Africa to Europe, had visited with the Queen and the royal children, had suffered illness and the loss of the man who had saved her. Now the child, barely eight years old, was being sent to yet another country.

Sarah had learned some geography. She knew where England was on the map, and where the continent of Africa was. But she didn't know where they were in her heart. She only knew that she was to make another long journey into the unknown.

1851

Back to Africa

THE *BATHURST* arrived at Freetown on the nineteenth of June, 1851, after thirty-three days at sea. The voyage had been difficult, with rough waters and poor, cramped accommodations aboard the steamer. Compared to the bustling dockside in England, the sleepy port of Sierra Leone, with its small fishing vessels and equally small ferries, seemed more than a world away. But at the Church Missionary

Society school there was an excited air of expectation as they awaited the little girl in whom the Queen herself had taken an interest. Reverend Henry Venn, the head of the missions in Africa, had written to the school about Sarah and of the royal concern in her.

Reverend Venn, a strong and dynamic man, had often clashed with some members of the Church Missionary Society. He wanted the missions in Africa to be run by the natives of the country they were in. He was also determined to bring education to young girls as well as boys, thinking that the well-being of girls would often determine the strength of the family. Eventually, he would have an important influence on Sarah's life.

The students of the Female Institution, which Sarah was to attend, came largely from Freetown and nearby villages. African parents who wanted their girls to take their places in the expanding African world knew that education would give them that chance. But for most of the students there was a fee required to attend the school. An African family that wanted to send their child to the institution had to provide the small amount of

A STREET IN FREETOWN, SIERRA LEONE

money necessary and also give up the benefit they could have gained from the child's labor. A few of the children attended the school free, supported by donations to the Church Missionary Society.

But there were important cultural differences between the English and their African hosts. The missionaries often had a low regard for the Africans. They considered the native religions "primitive," and their writings often

referred to blacks as savages. While many African women, depending on which people they were from, wore dresses that covered them from the shoulder to their ankles, others did not cover the tops of their bodies. The missionaries wanted them to wear European clothing, or at least some form of African dress that conformed with English taste. The young African girls in the girls' school were being outfitted in English dresses, English bonnets, and were taught English hymns. For African children, attending the missionary school meant giving up most of their own culture.

Miss Sass, the head of the school, personally welcomed Sarah. Sarah's luggage, which included her clothing as well as a number of gifts from the Queen, was unloaded and put into a cart to be carried to Miss Sass's home. There were no fancy coaches in Freetown as there had been in London, and the streets were not paved.

While most of the girls at the school slept in a large dormitory, Sarah was settled into her own room. Sarah's photograph of the Queen was put on the wall. And thus her new life in Sierra Leone began.

In the mornings, the streets of Freetown would be busy with women carrying bundles of yams, okra, and cassava on their heads. Smells of cooking food drifted through the streets, and the cries of people selling fish and vegetables punctuated the heavy, humid air. British ships were anchored off shore along with fishing boats and commercial ships. During the rainy season, children walking to the school would have to avoid the puddles to keep their shoes dry. In fact, many of the native people working or living in Sierra Leone went without shoes. It was a far cry from the England Sarah had known.

Sarah was introduced to the other girls. Abigail Crowther was an older girl who had been to England with her father, the Reverend Samuel Crowther, who was to become the first African bishop of the Niger River region. Most of the others had never been out of Sierra Leone. A few of the girls had been, like Sarah, captured in the slave raids and rescued by British ships patrolling the African coast.

Sarah, according to missionary records, was clearly a favored student. Miss Sass became her unofficial guardian, taking her on picnics and to nearby markets. The teachers at the school treated Sarah as special, allowing her to dress in the clothing she had brought from England or what was made for her from material sent by the Queen, while the other children wore simple dresses that were made by either the students or staff.

At age eight, Sarah could talk about her visits to Windsor Castle, and of having tea with the royal children.

She could tell the teachers at the school about her discussions with Queen Victoria and Prince Albert. She had been places and seen things that the teachers could only dream about.

Sarah did well with her schoolwork. She had spent a year in England, speaking and writing English, and had

CHURCH MISSIONARY FEMALE INSTITUTION
REPORT NO. 3, LIST OF CLASSES AND TIME

Time	Monday	Tuesday	Wednesday	Thursday	Friday	Saturday
6	Hour of Rising	"	"	"	"	"
7-8	Study	"	"	"	"	"
8	Prayers	"	"	"	"	"
9-11	Scripture Lessons	"	"	"	"	"
11-12	Study	Globes	Arithmetic	Grammar	Geography	"
12-1	Knitting	Sewing	Darning	Sewing	Marking	Mending
1-2	Reading	"	"	"	"	"
6-7	Study	"	"	"	"	"
8	Prayers	"	"	"	"	"

taken private lessons with the Forbes family. She could already write and read from the text they used, *Murray's English Grammar*. She was also learning to play the piano, which seemed easy to her.

Miss Sass reported on Sarah's progress to Reverend Venn who, in turn, reported to Mr. Phipps that Sarah was doing very well with the strict schedule.

Sarah eagerly awaited the weekly arrival of the steamer that brought mail from England. She received letters

❖ THE MAIL STEAMER IN FREETOWN'S HARBOR, 1800S ❖

from Mary Forbes, and letters and gifts from Queen Victoria.

During the fall of 1851, the year Sarah was sent to Sierra Leone, Commander Forbes's two volume work, *Dahomey and the Dahomans*, was published in England. A copy of this work, with her story and picture, must have been sent to the Female Institution, further enhancing Sarah's favored position.

At times, Miss Sass and another teacher, Miss Wilkinson, who had both come from England to teach in the mission school, would discuss who among the girls would be a good teacher, and who would not.

Their idea of the native girls becoming teachers and showing the other Africans how to live and to read the Bible was a strong motivation for the white women. Yet it often seemed, to the native Africans, that the real purpose of the school was to turn African girls into models of Christian English girls. The students were encouraged to maintain individual flower gardens. They were also taught to make and mend clothes designed in the English fashion, skills that were hardly needed in West Africa.

And yet the African girls could never be English girls. Sierra Leone was not England, and the white missionaries rarely considered the black girls equals.

Still, whenever visitors came to Miss Sass's house, Sarah, who had learned to speak very proper English, would be presented formally. Visitors would want to know about her, to understand why the Queen had been so drawn to her, and to judge whether she were deserving of that honor. Undoubtedly, Miss Sass felt the pressure of educating the young girl. While the other girls were learning the fundamentals of reading and writing, Sarah was being introduced to French. She was being trained to take her place in English upper-class society.

The Queen continued to send gifts of games and toys to Sarah. She also sent children's books, which Sarah read eagerly. But the girls in the books were all white, often with blonde hair and blue eyes. When Sarah looked in the mirror, she saw the face of a slim black girl with dark eyes and hair. She thought of Mrs. Forbes, how very fair she was, and of Princess Alice, who was very close to Sarah's age. It had been Queen Victoria herself who had called Sarah a princess. Yet how different she and Princess Alice were.

Sarah wrote to Her Majesty on a regular basis. The Queen is reported, in the records of the Church Missionary Society, as being quite pleased with Sarah's progress.

Besides the Queen's presents, Mr. Phipps was sending money directly to the school for Sarah's expenses. Reverend Venn expressed his surprise that new furniture had been purchased for Sarah, and asked Miss Sass whether the expenditure had been suggested by Her Majesty, Mr. Phipps, or some other person. Reverend Venn was not clear about Sarah's status. Was she to be treated as royalty? Would she always be under the protection of the Queen? In England there was a class system that few people ever questioned. There was an upper class headed by the royalty, a small middle class, which included merchants, military officers, and some of the clergy, and a large lower class. Sarah was being treated as an upper-class person despite the fact that she was without her own fortune.

A listing of Sarah's expenses appeared in the Church Missionary records:

	POUNDS	SHILLINGS	PENCE
Colored muslin		7	0
Print for 4 frocks	1	0	0
24 Yards long cloth		14	6
1 Doz. cotton hose	1	4	0
2 P. checked muslin	1	18	8
14 Reels cotton		2	0
Mantle (*black silk*)	1	8	0
Work for frocks		17	8
Mittens & gloves		7	5
Ribbon		1	$^{1}/_{2}$
2 Bonnets	1	7	$8\,^{1}/_{2}$
4 Aprons	1	0	0
Paper & envelopes		2	0
Pomatum (*hair dressing*)		4	0
Soap		3	0

The total for Sarah's supplies, sent to her by mail, was

the equivalent of over five weeks' salary for an average poor family living in England!

～～∽

On the twenty-fourth of May, 1852, Sarah was allowed to host a tea party for thirty-three girls in honor of the Queen's birthday. One can imagine all of these young African girls — Kru, Mendi, Egba, Egbado, and others — having tea and then being led by a nine-year-old in the singing of "God Save the Queen."

> *God save our gracious Queen*
> *Long live our noble Queen*
> *God save the Queen!*
> *Send her victorious*
> *Happy and glorious*
> *Long to reign over us*
> *God save the Queen!*

But while Sarah's life seemed secure and pleasant at the Female Institution, there was news that had to prove disturbing to her. King Gezo had repeatedly attacked Abeokuta, a Yoruba city a short distance from her old village. The Church Missionary Society was trying to establish a mission in the city and Abigail Crowther's father had been there during one of the raids. He had written to the mission offices describing King Gezo's attack and the successful defense of the city. Sarah breathed a sigh of relief, but was upset to know that King Gezo was still about. The distance from Sierra Leone to Dahomey did not seem long enough on the map in their geography book.

While the news of King Gezo's assault on Abeokuta was a matter of concern for all of the missionaries, for Sarah it brought back dreadful memories. There had been talk about some of the girls at the school becoming missionaries and living in cities like the one that had been raided. But Sarah thought she would never be brave enough to face another attack by King Gezo.

News of what was happening in West Africa came most often from men like Samuel Crowther and other mission-aries who stopped in Sierra Leone for a few days rest from their travels. Distinguished visitors to Sierra Leone were always shown the schools, including the Female Institution, as it was in these schools that Reverend Venn thought the future of the continent was being formed. One such visitor was James P. L. Davies, who was both a missionary and a businessman who promoted trading along the west coast of Africa. He was introduced to Sarah when he visited the Female Institution. She was the institution's star pupil, and he was pleased to meet the youngster. Years later, when it mattered, Sarah would hardly remember what he looked like.

All of the reports from the institution show that Sarah continued doing well in school as the years passed. She was busy with her French lessons from Miss Sass, as well as with piano and singing lessons. But there is no indication that she was either truly happy or unhappy in the African school. Then, quite suddenly, after four years of schooling in Sierra Leone, the institution received a letter from the palace concerning Sarah.

In the report of September 29, 1855, Miss Wilkinson wrote:

In May I had a letter from the Hon Mrs. Phipps,
requesting me to send Sally Forbes Bonetta at once to
England by her Majesty's command. Having consult-
ed our Missionary brethren, who agreed with me that
the command was too preemptory to admit of delay I
immediately made preparations and on the 23rd of
June Sally sailed for England under the care of Rev.
E. Dicker.

Why did the Queen have Sarah sent back to England so suddenly? What had Sarah written to her? One can only think that Sarah had, for whatever reason, become unhappy in Sierra Leone and told the Queen that she wanted to return to England. Since the Queen believed Africa would be better for Sarah's health, it must have been a very convincing letter.

In her report Miss Wilkinson refers to Sarah as Sally Forbes Bonetta. Throughout her life Sarah would offer different names for herself. Sometimes she refers to herself as Sarah Forbes Bonetta, sometimes as Sarah Bonetta Forbes. There are times when she signs her letters Etta, and even Ina. It is as if the young African girl returning to England were still trying to find a place and an identity for herself.

England Once Again

On Saturday, the twenty-third of June, 1855, Sarah was at the docks in Sierra Leone. The teachers and some of the students were there to see her off. Miss Sass checked and rechecked the luggage, making sure that all of the presents the Queen had sent Sarah were packed and taken on board. Reverend Dicker, an English missionary who had taught at the Female Institution, and his wife were to accompany Sarah to

England and they, too, said their good-byes at the dock. Rowers, strong black men who spoke a Creole that Sarah only partially understood, took Sarah and the Dickers in a small boat to the steamer off shore. From the dock, Miss Sass and Miss Wilkinson watched Sarah bravely wave good-bye to everyone she was leaving behind.

Aboard the steamer, Sarah settled into her small cabin. It contained only a cot, a plain table, a waste pot, and a chair. On the table she placed her Bible, to be read every day on the journey, and her photograph of Queen Victoria.

Once loaded, the steamship lifted anchor and headed toward the open sea. Soon, the dark mountains looming over the inland of Sierra Leone became less distinct. Turning away from the land that had been her home for four years, and the continent of her birth, Sarah felt the wind in her face as she began the trip back to England.

~⁓~

Throughout her stay in Sierra Leone, Sarah had seen British ships bring in Africans caught up in the slave trade. Commander Forbes had been involved in breaking up the slave forts that had once held the captives of the famous ship *La Amistad*. Now she was again on board a ship herself. Whatever she did, it seemed there were always dangers. But she was glad to be returning to England.

She was headed into a new adventure. Would she live with Mary Forbes? Would she ever again know anyone with the kindness and strength of Commander Forbes? Whatever happened, she thought, she would do well. After all, she was twelve now, no longer a mere child.

The trip seemed endless, and with the barely tolerable food Sarah knew she was losing weight. She prayed she would not get ill. When at last the activity of the crew told her that they had arrived in England, she was over-joyed. The landing was more hectic than Sarah remem-bered from her first trip to Gravesend. There was an air of excitement as lines were thrown onto the dock and secured. Mrs. Dicker accompanied her off the ship.

The dockside teemed with people carrying bundles to load onto the ships at anchor or onto the waiting line of horse-drawn carts. Soon Sarah was in a carriage, which shook and rattled its way toward London. The city itself seemed a study in chaos. It was summertime, and the streets overflowed with people calling out their wares, with horses and carriages, and workmen weaving their way through crowds of shoppers. By the time they arrived at the Church Missionary Society offices off Waterloo Street, it was late in the day and Sarah was exhausted. She had made the voyage not only from one continent to another but from an African culture to an English culture that seemed more than a lifetime away. It was her second such trip. This time, at least, she knew a little more of what to expect.

Mrs. Forbes was now a widow with four small children to care for, and had moved from Windsor to Scotland where she would be near her family. Having Sarah in her care would have been too much for her. It had been arranged by the Queen for Sarah to stay with a family, the Schoens, in Palm Cottage, Gillingham.

Although her teacher, Miss Wilkinson, had received the letter commanding that Sarah be returned to

England in May 1855, her return had been planned by the Queen since the beginning of the year. On the twenty-seventh of February Mrs. Phipps had written to Mrs. Schoen saying the Queen did not approve of Sarah's situation in Africa. Would she be willing to take charge of the young girl? Thirty-nine-year-old Elizabeth Schoen had earlier discussed Sarah at length with Mrs. Phipps and had found her story enchanting. Yes, she would be pleased to include Sarah in her home.

Arrangements were made with Mrs. Schoen and a budget for Sarah's upkeep was established by the Queen.

Reverend James Frederick Schoen was born in 1803. At the age of twenty-nine he had traveled to Africa and had done missionary work there from 1832 to 1847. Together with Samuel Crowther, whose daughter Sarah had known, he had explored the regions around the Niger River. After contracting a fever in 1847, he was forced to leave Africa to preserve his health. In 1855, England was at war with Russia. The Crimean War produced many casualties, and Reverend Schoen was the chaplain at Melville Hospital near his home.

THE REVEREND JAMES SCHOEN

The Schoen family lived in a modest house on Canterbury Road in Gillingham, an hour's trip by rail from London. There were few other homes nearby, and from the hill on which their own Palm Cottage sat, the neighboring fields could be seen for miles around. In 1855, when Sarah arrived at the Schoen home, there were seven children in the house. Of these, Frederick Schoen was the closest in age to Sarah. Beside Mr. and Mrs.

Schoen and the Schoen children, the household also consisted of a twenty-three-year-old cook and a sixteen-year-old nursemaid.

Mary Forbes was pleased at the Queen's choice of homes for Sarah and wrote to Mrs. Schoen.

Dear Mrs. Schoen,

I am charmed to hear you are to train up the little Princess. I am sure you will take care and not let her be made a show of, which makes girls so conceited. It will be very spoiling for her if the Queen takes too much notice of her.

MARY FORBES

The adults around Sarah understood what the special relationship between the young black girl and the Queen meant. Mrs. Forbes was worried that Sarah might become conceited or spoiled. But a letter from Mrs. Phipps to Mrs. Schoen shortly after Sarah's return to England signaled that the girl was to resume her visits to the Queen at St. James's Palace, another royal residence.

After one such visit in December 1855, the Queen wrote in her diary:

> *Saw Sally Forbes, the negro girl, whom I have had educated; she is immensely grown and has a lovely slim figure.*

Queen Victoria always worried about her weight and advised her daughters to watch theirs. But while the Queen had to worry about her waistline, this was not the case for most of the poor children who lived throughout England and Ireland. A good idea of how privileged Sarah was to be under the Queen's protection may be had by considering the situation of some of the poor children in England at the time.

When Sarah returned to London there were thousands of children her own age living in terrible conditions. Many were homeless, and many went to bed hungry each night.

Mother has been dead just a year this month; she took cold at the washing and it went to her chest; she was only bad a fortnight; she suffered great pain, and, poor thing, she used to fret dreadful, as she lay ill, about me, for she knew she was going to leave me. She used to plan how I was to do when she was gone. She made me promise to try to get a place and keep from the streets if I could, for she seemed to dread them so much. When she was gone I was left in the world without a friend. I am quite alone, I have no relation at all, not a soul belonging to me. For three months I went about looking for a place, as long as my money lasted, for mother told me to sell our furniture to keep me and get me clothes. I could have got a place, but nobody would have me without a character, and I knew nobody to give me one. I tried very hard to get one, indeed I did; for I thought of all mother had said to me about going into the streets. At last, when my money was just gone, I met a young woman in the street, and I asked her to tell me where I could get a lodging. She told me to come with her, she would show me a respectable lodging house for women and girls. I went, and I have been there ever since. The women in the house advised me to take to flower-selling, as I could get nothing else to do.

— FROM *LONDON LABOUR AND THE LONDON POOR*

BY HENRY MAYHEW

Sarah took immediately to her new home and to Elizabeth Schoen. She began to refer both to Mrs. Schoen and to Mrs. Phipps as "Mama," but it was Mrs. Schoen with whom she would form the stronger emotional tie.

By 1856, Sarah had settled into the daily routines of the Schoen family. Central to that life at Palm Cottage was religion. Reverend Schoen was deeply involved in church activities and most of the people with whom the family associated were connected with the Church of England.

Reverend Schoen was also a scholar, specializing in the study of languages. He had learned many African languages and wrote articles and books about them. The atmosphere in the Schoen household was studious but

❖ A STREET SCENE IN POOR VICTORIAN LONDON ❖

lively. The children were taught at home, and Sarah continued her education with the older Schoen children.

Sarah showed an abiding interest in all the members of the Schoen family throughout her life. They were as

SARAH FORBES BONETTA, 1856

much her true family as any other group of people had ever been.

Throughout this time, Sarah's health was still delicate, and she was frequently ill. Mrs. Phipps, probably at the Queen's command, made sure to send her warm clothing. One letter asks if Sarah would need a fire in her room while visiting the castle, which was known to be drafty. On her visits to the Queen in particular she was to be dressed well.

WINDSOR

THURSDAY

Dear Mrs. Schoen,

    I have sent dear Sally a handsome dress & a pr. of sleeves & when she comes to London I will give her a scarf edged with white fringe & then if we give her a pink bonnet I think she will do, but to keep her warm she had better wear an under garment....

M. A. PHIPPS

Sometimes Sarah would see the Queen alone, and at

least on one occasion she was brought to a "Drawing Room," during which time the Queen would be available for brief meetings with foreign diplomats, businessmen, and some members of the public. It was a great honor to be allowed to watch these proceedings.

Visits to the Queen would often involve an examination of Sarah's "work," which meant a review of her progress in learning. In his book *Dahomey and the Dahomans*, Commander Forbes had written of Sarah:

> She is far in advance of any white child of her age, in aptness of learning, and strength of mind and affection....

Queen Victoria had made it a practice to bring members of other nationalities and races to the palace and often expressed a willingness to treat them as equals, a progressive way of thinking at the time. She saw in Sarah a young African girl who, once given the advantage of a good education, would prove to be a worthy contributor to the British Empire.

Mrs. Phipps frequently refers to Sarah's intellectual progress and the Queen's pleasure with it:

ST. JAMES PALACE

TUESDAY

Dear Mrs. Schoen,

We all think dear Sally very much improved in her mind. She will remain here till Tuesday & is then going to visit Dr. & Mrs. Brown & after that Mrs. Forbes's Family. So in case of her being absent a Month I think it would be better to send what more clothes you consider necessary with a list & as her dressing gown has been forgotten kindly order that to be sent also & all things direct here to me....

Yrs. Truly,

M. A. PHIPPS

As part of her studies in Sierra Leone, Sarah had learned to sew. She used this skill to make a pair of slippers for Prince Albert. The Queen was so impressed with this that she asked Sarah to make a pair for her!

And as pleased as the Queen was, Sarah seemed just as pleased with her life in England. Her letters to Mama Schoen reveal nothing about her thoughts on her African heritage.

WINDSOR CASTLE

NOVEMBER 13TH

Dear Mama,

I arrived yesterday afternoon at Windsor. Lady Phipps met me at the station in the chariot with Mrs. Mallett's little girl Eva. Charlie is much better. It seems he had been very ill. Albert is at home and is a very gentlemanly little fellow. Harriet and Col. Phipps are in Norfolk so I got dear Mama Phipps all to myself. Was it not kind of the Queen — she sent to know if I had arrived last night as she wishes to see me some morning. I am going out in the Pony carriage with Mama presently. She asked me if you brought me to London and when she found that we had had to wait said we might have gone to St.

James's Palace to wait. Col. Cavendish came to see
Lady P. last night, she introduced me to him.
With love, I remain always
Affectionately Yours,

S. Forbes Bonetta

Charlie and Albert are Mrs. Phipps's boys. Harriet is Mrs. Phipps's daughter, and Col. Phipps is, of course, her husband. St. James's Palace is located in London, and Mrs. Phipps had suggested that Sarah and Mrs. Schoen stay there while waiting for their train connections to Windsor. These were the people and places in Sarah's world, and their doings and concerns fill her letters. She had lost her own family and the Schoens had replaced them in her heart. It seemed only natural that she would come to adopt their values and their culture as her own.

The Schoen family, with a servant girl and a nurse-maid, was clearly doing quite well in Victorian England, but Sarah herself, with her direct connection to the

Queen, lived a life that would have been remarkable for even an upper-class young woman.

~~~

Sarah returned to England at a very exciting time. The English novelist Charles Dickens had just written *Little Dorritt*, Charles Darwin was working on *The Origin of Species*, Florence Nightingale was saving lives in the ongoing Crimean War, and in the United States the novel *Uncle Tom's Cabin* by Harriet Beecher Stowe was fanning the flames of dissent that would eventually lead to the American Civil War.

Sarah's letters do not deal with the great issues of the day and, in all probability, neither did her conversations with the young Princes and Princesses at Windsor Castle. They may well have centered around the upcoming marriage of Princess Victoria.

The Princess Royal had been only fourteen in 1855 when a young man expressed interest in having her for his bride. The man was Prince Frederick William of Prussia. Marriages among European royalty were often arranged when the bride and groom were far too young to marry. It would be nice if the couple loved each other or grew to love each other, but there were other factors to be considered. Were the couple of equal rank? Were their countries on friendly terms? If not, would the marriage help or hurt the relations between the countries? Princess Victoria had a fondness for Frederick, and when the young man expressed interest, the Queen was delighted. A formal proposal was not to be made at once, as the Princess was too young, but an understanding was reached. The official announcement was finally made in 1857, and Sarah, too, was pleased.

OSBORNE

12TH

My dear Mrs. Schoen,

The Queen has desired me to send dear Sally a picture of Prince F of Prussia & you may expect it this week & if Sally wishes to have it framed kindly get it done for her —

M. A. PHIPPS

Sarah's relationships with the royal children seemed always to be quite good. She refers to the Prince of Wales as "Bertie," and one letter mentions her correspondence with Princess Alice. But the most public show of her connection with the royal family occurred at the wedding of the Princess Royal.

A command has been received from her Majesty for Sarah Bonetta Forbes, the young African Princess...to be present to witness the marriage ceremony of the Princess Royal. Her Majesty has manifested her thoughtful care towards the Princess by forwarding her within the last few days a supply of dresses and other requisites suitable to be worn on the occasion.

— *The Illustrated London News*

The marriage between Princess Victoria and Prince Frederick William of Prussia took place on Monday, the twenty-fifth of January, 1858. There were approximately 800 guests at the wedding, many of whom came from

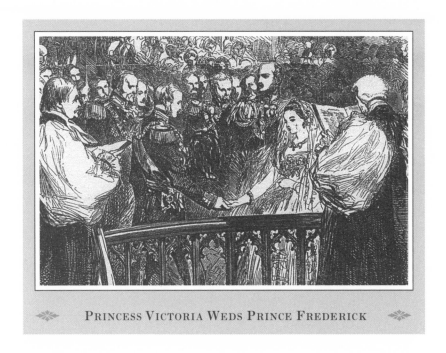

PRINCESS VICTORIA WEDS PRINCE FREDERICK

Germany, France, and other European countries. The invitations extended to British subjects were limited to royalty, special friends of the royal families, and other important British and European persons. All of London was in a festive mood.

Regent Street, Piccadilly, St. James's Street, Bond Street, Oxford Street, the Strand, and Fleet Street were the thoroughfares in which the best displays were made. The clubhouses were illuminated with devices in gas, and those connected with the military and naval services were especially remarkable for the rich and elaborate nature of their decorations. The "Army and Navy," at the corner of St. James's Square, in Pall Mall, maintained its superiority by exhibiting a magnificent device, in which the arms of the two services were blended.

— *THE ILLUSTRATED LONDON NEWS*

The following account of the dresses worn by the Royal and illustrious personages who took part in the marriage ceremony appeared in *The Illustrated London News:*

The Princess Royal's bridal dress was of white moiré antique, the body trimmed with Honiton lace, and a bouquet of orange flowers and myrtle; the petticoat trimmed with three flounces of Honiton lace, wreathed with orange and myrtle, and the train of white moiré antique, lined with satin, bordered with a ruche of white satin ribbons, Honiton lace, and a wreath of orange flowers and myrtle to correspond with the dress; diamond necklace, earrings, and brooch, the Prussian Order of Louisa, and a Portuguese order. The headdress a wreath of orange flowers and myrtle; the veil of Honiton lace, to correspond with the dress. The design of the lace is alternate medallions of the rose, shamrock, and thistle, with a rich ground of the leaves of the rose, shamrock, and thistle.

The Princess Alice wore a dress of white lace over rich satin trimmed with corn-flowers and daisies. The Princess wore a wreath of the same flowers round the head.

The Princesses Helena and Louisa wore dresses similar to that of the Princess Alice, with corn-flowers and daisies in the hair.

The Prince of Wales, Prince Alfred, Prince Arthur, and Prince Leopold wore the Highland dress.

Prince Frederick William wore a Prussian General's uniform, a dark blue tunic, with gold embroidery on the collar and cuffs, a gold aiguillette on the right shoulder, a silver sash, and white kerseymere trousers.

Princess Victoria's marriage was arranged when the Princess was only fourteen years old, and she was married shortly after her seventeenth birthday. Victorian ladies "came out" into public life at seventeen or eighteen and actively began the search for husbands. For those women who were in the upper class, with either private fortunes or titles, there were few other choices. The better jobs were reserved for men, and it was not looked on as proper for a lady of the period to work even as a clerk. The few jobs that women were allowed usually had to do with religious work such as missionaries, and some teaching positions. This, of course, did not hold true for the working class, in which women often did work as street sellers, maids, or housekeepers.

The question was, what would Sarah do? She did not

have an independent income or an English title. In 1858, the year of Princess Victoria's wedding, both Sarah and Princess Alice were fifteen. A number of young princes from Europe were already being considered as possible husbands for Princess Alice.

A good marriage was considered the most important event in an Englishwoman's life and girls were expected to be thinking of marriage when they reached their teenage years. Young women of the time liked to scan the newspapers to see announcements of upcoming weddings of friends and relatives. But there were other stories in the newspapers of 1858 and 1859 that Sarah might have noticed with great interest.

In 1859, the relationship between the United States and England grew tense. The cause of the tension was the growing problems between the North and the South in America. The South, which supplied much of the cotton used by English industries, was seeking the support of Great Britain in case of war. Central to the American conflict was the subject of slavery. Prince Albert was the head of the British and Foreign Anti-Slavery Society and slavery had already been outlawed throughout the empire. In England, black Americans such as Frederick Douglass, William Wells Brown, and William and Ellen Craft, had lectured against the slave trade and had sought and received British support. Although it is not evident from her letters that Sarah ever met any of these figures, it is clear that at least some of them knew of her. William Craft, who escaped from southern slavery with his wife, Ellen, mentioned Sarah in a speech as an example of black accomplishments. While there were a great many English involved in anti-slavery movements, those around Sarah were involved in the missionary effort to spread the teachings of the Church of England. The Schoens' oldest daughter, Harriet, married a missionary in 1858. Sarah had been a bridesmaid at the wedding.

In 1860 Sarah was still living with the Schoen family. She spent a great deal of her time visiting friends in London, Windsor, and sometimes Moniack Castle, Scotland, where Mary Forbes now lived. Her visits to the Queen continued, and her friendship with Princess Alice deepened. In October 1860, Sarah traveled to London with Frederick, the oldest of Reverend Schoen's sons. Her letter home is chatty and mentions her correspondence with Princess Alice.

My dear Mama,

We arrived safely last evening. Mr. Vidal met us at the station before Hailsham. We reached the Vicarage at 10 minutes after 7. It was fully 2 hours ride in the train from London Bridge. I have only 10/6 pence from the 2 pounds you gave us before we started. Besides the tickets I used 3 pence for some cakes and 6 pence for visiting cards and 6 pence this morning for stamps. Will you send me some more money please.... I hope Colonel Phipps will not be angry at my traveling expenses.

Shall I write to Lady Phipps to let her know that I

am here? Has Fanny Pratt written to you since their precipitate retreat, to say how they performed their journey to London. When I see her won't I give Fanny a lecture for their shameful and shabby behavior. I hope if I do go to see her that Thomas Spitsburg will not be there at all, otherwise I shall wish myself further. We arrived too late last night to write, for the post leaves at 6 o'clock and we did not arrive till past 7 o'clock. Mrs. Vidal is rather anxious to see the Princess Alice's letter, it is in my desk. Will you please tell Miss Norris how sorry I am at having brought her thimble with me. My love to her. Mr. and Mrs. Vidal desire their very kind regards to you and with much love to yourself and kisses to the dear children and regards to Dad.

Always yours affectionately,

S. F. BONETTA

Sarah doesn't mention what was in Princess Alice's letter, but the seventeen-year-old princess had been recently engaged to twenty-three-year-old Prince Louis of Hesse-Darmstadt.

A month later, the twenty-second of November, we find Sarah again at Windsor Castle.

The Queen's cousin had died and the Queen had decided that the castle should go into mourning. This meant that certain rituals would have to be observed. Mourning periods always lasted for a specific time, depending on how important the person was who had died. Men had to wear black armbands and women were supposed to dress completely in black. When Sarah arrived at the palace, she did not know that they were in mourning.

WINDSOR CASTLE

NOVEMBER 22, 1860

My dear Mama,

I am now writing to you at 10 o'clock at night in haste to ask you to get my black silk dress altered and retrimmed as the Court is in mourning and I dare not appear before the Queen in colours. I go to Mrs. Brown's before on Saturday & do not in the least know when the Queen will send for me, not before

Sunday I am sure as she knows that Lady Phipps is not well. Could you possibly get Mrs. Foster to alter & retrim my dress & have it sent to Windsor by Wednesday morning early or Tuesday night which would be best I think. <u>Do try</u> if you can possibly manage it. I should like the skirt lengthened by 2 inches at the back & 1 in front. The bottom of the dress I should like bound with black velvet nice & deep, nearly as deep as this envelope. The body will want something done to it under the arms and the sleeves a little more trimmed with some of the bows down the front.

Bye the bye, I should like some velvet buttons all down the whole dress (though it is not <u>absolutely</u> <u>necessary</u>). I should not in the least like to borrow a dress from Harriet to see the Queen in. She would not like it at all. Please send me a pair of black kid gloves.

I should have written for my dress before but thought I might borrow one. Since I've seen her my mind's altered. I am so sorry to hurry you so much (but Lady P. ought to have told about the Court being in mourning before I came). I'll pay for the gloves. The dress had better come in a paper parcel (being a plain skirt it won't hurt) to me directed. My name, Dr. Brown's, Windsor. It will be sure to find me there.

Harriet & Col. P. came home this evening. She enquired after you & is very kind. With best love to all, yourself of course included.

Yours affectionately,

S.F. Bonetta

I have been writing this in my bedroom when everyone else is asleep. Please send in the parcel the black lace off my green bonnet & the black trimming off the one I brought with me. Don't forget them please.

1860

The Decision

In November of 1860, when Sarah wrote to her adopted mother from the castle at Windsor, she seemed to have nothing on her mind beyond the immediate business of her visit and the proper mourning clothes. Sarah and Princess Alice were friends and undoubtedly shared secrets. Princess Alice had just become engaged that June. But when Sarah visited the palace in November she had a secret of her own. Although she had not taken it seriously, she, too, had received a proposal of marriage.

James Pinson Labulo Davies was thirty-one years of age. Born in West Africa, he received his early education in the school run by the Church Missionary Society. He had been trained to work as a ship's captain but his interests were more in missionary work than in the strictly business aspects of shipping. Reverend Henry Venn, of the Church Missionary Society's operations in West Africa, thought highly of Davies. He had encouraged Davies to start his own business and to help others as part of his conviction that progress in Africa depended on native Africans developing their own economy. Davies did expand his business holdings but also engaged in missionary work.

James Davies had actually seen Sarah at the Female Institution in Sierra Leone when she studied there. He also knew of the Queen's interest in the young girl. When they had first met, Sarah was only a child and Davies was in his twenties and already married.

In February of 1860, his wife, Matilda Davies, had

died after a brief illness. A few months later he wrote to Sarah. He introduced himself again, and after explaining about the death of his wife, he asked Sarah if she would consider marrying him.

Did Sarah and Princess Alice discuss marriage? Did Sarah mention that she had received a proposal from Davies? There is no indication of how Mrs. Phipps found out about the proposal, but she brought up the subject to Mrs. Schoen in a letter at this time. Had Sarah actually received this proposal? Was it serious?

Queen Victoria was Sarah's great protector and most valued friend in England. It was the Queen who paid Sarah's bills, who saw to her needs, and who continually considered her well-being. But the Queen also had definite views on a woman's place in society. She believed that women should marry and be a help and comfort to their husbands.

Sarah had taken the tentative proposal lightly. She did not know Mr. Davies that well, and had no particular interest in getting to know him better. But both the Queen and Mrs. Phipps were interested in the idea of

HER MAJESTY, THE QUEEN

marriage as a way of "settling" Sarah. Who was the man who had proposed to Sarah and what were his prospects? Would he make a match that the Queen would find acceptable? The Queen had Mr. Phipps investigate the matter.

Charles Phipps wrote a detailed letter to Reverend

Venn, asking about Davies's qualities, his character, and his finances. Would he be, in other words, a candidate for marriage to Sarah of whom the Queen would approve?

Sarah had been enjoying her life at Palm Cottage with the Schoens. Mr. Schoen was a recognized scholar in African languages and Mrs. Schoen was the kindest woman Sarah had ever met. When Mr. Phipps received a favorable report from Reverend Venn about James Davies, and had discussed it with the Queen, the question was asked directly to Sarah. Would she marry Mr. Davies? Her immediate reaction was no, she did not want to marry Mr. Davies.

The Queen had known Sarah for most of her life. She had known her as a bright child, eager to learn and eager to please. She had seen her grow into a graceful and charming woman. She understood that young women wanted to marry for love, as she had loved and married Prince Albert. But she also understood that the role of women, at least in her times, was not always easy. A woman could not simply follow her heart. As long as Sarah was content with the Schoens, the Queen felt, she would not be willing to make a decision based on the practical considerations that Her Majesty thought necessary. It was decided to move Sarah from her home.

A letter was sent to Mrs. Schoen from the palace. Sarah was to go to the home of a Miss Welsh, a relative of Mrs. Phipps, in Brighton, some fifty miles away.

Sarah was devastated.

Brighton had been a small fishing village called Brighthelmstone for most of its existence. In 1784, the construction of the famous Royal Pavilion was begun there. The pavilion was designed as a resort home for the Prince of Wales. With the coming of the Prince and the pavilion, the fishing village became a popular place for holidays. Situated on the English Channel in southern England, it lent itself to the sport of sailing and pleasure boating as it had once done for fishing. By 1841, Brighthelmstone had become Brighton and was accessible by railroad.

Along the waterfront there are small shops designed

for the tourist trade. The town itself rises steeply above the Channel, affording a fine view from the homes facing eastward toward France. Summer sunsets over the English Channel are truly beautiful, and the early morning winter mists have a cold enchantment of their own. Sarah arrived in Brighton in the spring. She was hurt and confused by the sudden changes in her life.

Mrs. Phipps wrote that Sarah would be better off

marrying someone of her own race. This was not a problem for Sarah. The problem was that she did not want it to be James Davies, a man she had not chosen on her own to be her husband.

Sarah's despair at being moved to Brighton was more than a reaction to her separation from the Schoens or the pressure on her to consider marriage. Since she had been a small child there had been very few places in Sarah's life that she could have felt that she truly belonged. She certainly did not belong with the Dahomans who had killed her parents. On the ship sailing from West Africa to England she amused the white sailors, but she had not been one of them. And later at the missionary school in Sierra Leone she was, as the Queen's protégée, always different than the other girls.

With the Schoens in Chatham, visiting the Queen, going on pony rides with the royal children, attending state functions as an African princess far from her own country, she did not truly belong. Now she was being sent to Brighton to live with the Welsh family.

Sophie J. Welsh was listed as the head of the house-

hold. She was sixty-two years old. Also in the house was Barbara Simon, a seventy-three-year-old widow; William Welsh, their nephew; and two servants, Eliza Brewer, twenty-eight, and her nineteen-year-old sister, Jane

Brewer. It was suggested by Mrs. Phipps that Sarah could be a companion to the older ladies. It was an idea that Sarah did not like at all.

The letters from Mrs. Phipps to Sarah in Brighton asked about J.P.L. Davies. He had done all that he could to ensure his credentials were favorable to the Queen.

Sarah had thought about marriage. She wanted to love the man she married, to find him tall and handsome and noble. She wanted to be swept off her feet by the incredible romance of his proposal. To marry Mr. Davies meant to marry someone she didn't love.

She asked Mrs. Schoen, who knew she hated living in Brighton with Miss Welsh, what she should do.

CLARENCE HOUSE

EAST BOGNOR

SUSSEX

MAR 16TH /61

My dearest Mama,

I have been in a state of mental misery & indecision ever since your 2nd letter arrived yesterday. I should have sat down to write to you the moment it arrived, but remembered that you would have said "take time to consider." I shall now tell you truly what my thoughts & feelings are, with regard to Mr. Davies. You remember perhaps when he proposed a year ago, I said I could never either love or marry him, and I thought it impossible for us to make each other happy. Had I cared for him, age would never have come in the way of my decision. It would be wicked I think, were I to accept him, when there are others that I prefer. It is useless expecting perfection, but at the same time I do not feel that our two disposi-tions would mix well together. I don't feel a particle of love for him & never have done so, though now it is a year since he last asked me. What am I to do? Please tell me dear Mama & don't say "decide as you feel." I have prayed & asked for guidance but it doesn't come, & the feeling of perfect indifference to him returns with greater force. I am quite stupid & don't know what to do, because I know that there are many of my friends who would say accept him, as then you would

have a home & protector & not be obliged to stay at
Miss Welsh's for an indefinite time. Others would say
"He is a good man & though you don't care about
him now, will soon learn to love him." That, I believe,
I never could do. I know that the generality of people
would say he is rich & your marrying him would at
once make you independent, and I say "Am I to
barter my peace of mind for money?" No — never!
Yours affectionately,

ETTA

Sarah understood her position very well. But how could she make a clear decision, after finally finding some measure of long-sought inner peace with family and friends like the Schoens? How could she be happy moving away from that peace into the uncertainty of marriage with a man she did not really know, let alone love? To influence her decision, those around her had removed Sarah from Palm Cottage and her adopted family. What hurt her so was that she could be so easily commanded to go, a reminder that she did not belong anywhere in

England. She wrote in another letter that she would remain with Miss Welsh until she returned to Africa. It was the first time she mentioned Africa as a place to which she would eventually return. But in Brighton, with its charming houses overlooking the seaside, with its gay scenes of vacationers frolicking on the clean beaches, Sarah felt a crushing isolation.

❖ THE VIEW FROM CLIFTON HILL AS IT LOOKS TODAY ❖

The house in Brighton was situated high on Clifton Hill, and it must have been quite hard for Sarah, who had breathing difficulties, to negotiate the steep streets as she returned from the church below. One can feel the bitterness as she describes her discomfort:

My dearest Mama,

I kept my composure very well 'till I went into my desolate little pigsty alone, & then I had a regular outburst, which I tried hard to overcome. . . .

Don't worry yourself at my writing in this way, for I cannot help it. My head would burst I think if I sat thinking about it all. It ached fearfully last night & is playing the same game this morning.

Yours affectionately,

ETTA

That same spring, on the sixteenth of March, 1861, the Duchess of Kent, the Queen's mother, died. Sarah, heartbroken over her own situation, nevertheless wrote a letter of sympathy to the Queen.

Madam,

I was very grieved indeed to hear of the loss Your Majesty had sustained in the death of the Duchess of Kent and beg to offer my very sincere sympathy. I should have written to Your Majesty before but thought it would be intruding on your grief. I am now with Miss Welsh and hope to be happy here. Though I cannot help feeling very sorry to leave my dear kind friends Mr. & Mrs. Schoen, with whom I have resided since my return from Africa. I feel indeed very grateful to them for their unremitting kindness to me. I should be very pleased to show my gratitude to them in some way. They are, and have always been, such sincere friends to my poor Country. The state of affairs out there is very distressing to me. I feel deeply Your Majesty's kindness to & interest in me, and hope & trust that I shall never prove ungrateful for all that I have received from you. Hoping Madam, *that You and all the Royal Family are quite well,*

I remain

Ever yr. grateful & affectionate

S. Forbes Bonetta

Mrs. Phipps, in a letter to Mrs. Schoen, said that it would be appropriate for Sarah to dress in mourning clothes. What Sarah did not realize at the time was that Albert, the Prince Consort, was also in poor health. And, despite the sympathy and gratitude expressed to the Queen in her letter, Sarah still felt abandoned.

The months dragged by slowly. Sarah was miserable living away from her adopted family. In all of her life she had never found a permanent place to call home.

Sarah began to think more about what life with James P. L. Davies would mean. She also thought of what life in England would be for her without the Queen's support. What would she do, as an African woman, on her own? The Queen approved of Mr. Davies. He had the resources to support Sarah, and he had promised to treat her well. Reverend Henry Venn had approved of his character.

Sarah knew that Princess Victoria at age fourteen had agreed to marry Prince Frederick. Princess Alice was engaged to marry Prince Louis. The Queen's daughters were either married or about to be married. Sarah understood that the Queen wanted to settle all the young girls in her life.

Then, in December of 1861, Prince Albert died.

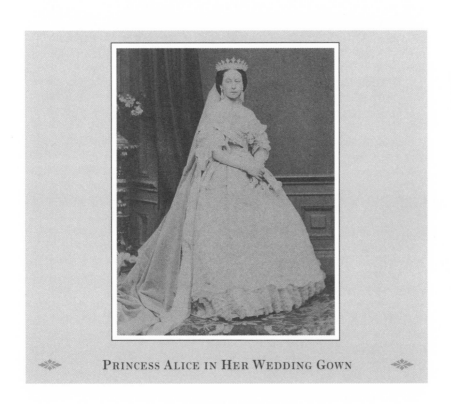

PRINCESS ALICE IN HER WEDDING GOWN

Within nine months Queen Victoria had lost both her mother and her beloved husband. All of England seemed drenched in sorrow. It echoed Sarah's own.

~~~~~~~~~~

Months later, on a sunny spring day in March 1862, Sarah was again at Windsor Castle. She had already written a letter to Mama Schoen in which she wondered who besides Mrs. Schoen really cared about her. She wandered about the castle grounds, thinking of what decision she should make. Perhaps Princess Alice walked with her.

"I enclose violets & primroses gathered under castle walls," she wrote, "they're so sweet."

Finally, and with great reluctance, Sarah had agreed to marry Mr. Davies.

Princess Alice's wedding had been planned for early 1862, but was postponed for six months due to the death of Prince Albert. It finally took place on the first of July, 1862. Sarah's wedding was planned for the next month, August 1862.

Sarah, c. 1862

1862

Sarah's Marriage

IT WAS THURSDAY, the fourteenth day of August, 1862. A light but steady rain dampened the streets of Brighton. In the distance the Channel was all but lost in the cold mist. Through the rain, horse-drawn carriages transported gaily dressed ladies and gentlemen the mile distance from the railroad station to St. Nicholas Church. The church itself, newly renovated, was already nearly filled.

ST. NICHOLAS CHURCH

What did Sarah feel? She was marrying a man she felt she could never truly love. But Mrs. Schoen had consoled her, and the royal family had made the wedding seem right. As she entered the church, there was an air of gaiety about her as the young women who had become her friends lined up for the procession. There were hugs and tears and last-minute adjustments to her gown. From the church interior, the sound of hymns filtered through the heavy wooden doors of the vestry. It was time for the ceremony to begin.

The first bridesmaids were African, the sister of James Davies and some other young African women attending schools in England. They were dressed in white gowns with red trim. The next four bridesmaids were English. They, too, wore white gowns, but with blue trim. A procession of very young girls followed.

Four English groomsmen accompanied James Davies to the front of the church, then stood while the bridesmaids came slowly down the aisle and formed a line across the front of the altar. It was then Sarah's turn.

Her gown was made of white silk with white trimmings. A wreath of orange blossoms sat lightly upon her head and held the white veil in place. By her side was Captain Forbes, the brother of the man who had rescued her and given her his name. It was he who gave the bride away. Reverend Venn and a Reverend Nichol from the Church Missionary Society assisted with the ceremonies.

There were hymns. Reverend Venn asked God to bless Sarah and James. The solemn vows of marriage were

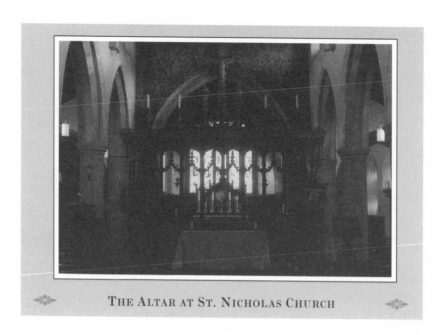

THE ALTAR AT ST. NICHOLAS CHURCH

exchanged. Sarah Forbes Bonetta became Sarah Forbes Bonetta Davies.

Later, there was cheering and congratulations and more tears as Sarah and her husband left the church. Outside, those who could not fit in the church cheered wildly as the couple, under a canopy of umbrellas, were ushered into a waiting carriage.

The wedding breakfast was held at West Hill Lodge. The Schoen family attended, as did the Forbes family.

The celebration lasted through the day. At four-thirty in the afternoon, Mr. and Mrs. Davies were driven to the railroad station from which they headed toward London.

Sarah had no choice in the life she would lead with James Davies. Her husband's work was in Africa, and soon the couple were on their way to Freetown. James Davies was to continue his business ventures, and Sarah would teach at the Female Institution.

The Church Missionary Society was still involved in a controversy over who should lead the schools and the mission stations. The English women who taught at the Female Institution in Freetown often considered them-selves culturally superior to the Africans they were

JAMES AND SARAH'S MARRIAGE CERTIFICATE

SARAH AND JAMES DAVIES

teaching. The class system in England was part of the ideology the missionaries brought with them, and the English teachers did not want to work under the direction of the native peoples. Alienation between the church and the Africans often resulted. Reverend Venn was among the few who believed that African teachers and clergy should be the ones to overcome this barrier.

The young African women who were eventually recruited as teachers had all been taught by English teachers and were expected not only to teach in English but also to pass on English values. As she had been nearly all of her life, nineteen-year-old Sarah was in a far different position from that of her peers. She had received an excellent education and had spent much of her young life in England. She knew as much about English culture as did the British teachers with whom she would work. She knew far more than they did of upper-class life and had a much greater range of experience.

As the wife of a successful businessman and as an acquaintance of the Queen she was in an extremely privileged position. Some of the teachers resented Sarah. She brought her own ideas as to what African girls needed to know, along with her own standards and the conviction that African women could be at least as effective as their English counterparts.

Sarah began to teach at the Female Institution at Sierra Leone and later at a similar school in Nigeria. Her letters indicate that she grew to be fond of Davies, who showed her a continual respect. Davies worked, often under the guidance of Reverend Venn, in building up commercial enterprises in the area. It was from these enterprises that Reverend Venn hoped to recruit the African leaders who would stabilize the area. James's business dealings, however, were not particularly successful as this letter from Sarah to Mrs. Schoen reveals.

APRIL 22, 1868

My dear Mama,

The fact is James is infinitely too good & kind to everybody, & he is not appreciated, & when he does anything, people detract him as a matter of course, & I think it his duty — to labor for the benefit of others

*but because they are all jealous of his position &
influence they are only too ready to cry him down &
abuse him, but thank you, that will not hurt him for
he knows in whom he has trusted & is safe....*

The obvious possibility was that Sarah would eventually head the school she once attended. But within months of her marriage she discovered she was pregnant.

Both James and Sarah were delighted that she was going to have a child. So was the royal family in England. Sarah wanted to name the child in honor of the royal family and, when the child was born a girl, she sought permission from the Queen to name her Victoria.

Yes, the word came from the palace. Queen Victoria would be delighted to have the child named in her honor and would even serve as the child's godmother.

This account appeared in the *Anti-Slavery Reporter*:

The Queen presented to her godchild a beautiful gold cup, with a salver, knife, fork and spoon, of the same precious metal, as a baptismal present. The cup and salver bear the following inscription. "To Victoria Davies, from her godmother, Victoria, Queen of Great Britain and Ireland, 1863."

After the birth of her daughter, Sarah moved to Lagos, on the coast of Africa just south of Badagry. During this time Queen Victoria saw very few people and made even fewer public appearances. It was as if the death of Prince Albert had so crushed her that she had lost the very will to live. But her relationship with Sarah, though much more distant now that Sarah lived most of the time in Africa, remained strong. A letter to Mrs. Schoen, whom Sarah always loved and stayed in contact with, describes a visit to Windsor Castle just before Christmas in 1867.

WINDSOR

DEC. 13TH, 1867

My dear Mama,

Please thank Cordelia for her letter. I cannot write two letters to each of you, so this one must do. We are well, but dear Victoria has a cough that she brought with her. We went to see the Queen on Monday & Vic was sent for again on Wednesday. She and Mr. Brown went up yesterday & returned with a beautiful doll. The conversation was all about Captain D & myself, so out of delicacy I was not asked to go up. They were all Charmed with the child, & the Queen gave her on Monday a dear gold locket with a brilliant on it & her likeness inside....

Victoria has just been to have her photo done for the Queen — tis to be colored.

You Cannot think how affected they all were with her, & yesterday Prince Leopold took possession of her & the Queen gave her sweets. No one saw her with Her Majesty yesterday except the Prince and Psses.

I hope all are well, I suppose it is terribly cold as usual.

Yours affectly,

I. S. F. DAVIES

The Queen noted Sarah's visit in her diary:

After luncheon saw Sally, now Mrs. Davies & her dear little child, far blacker than herself, called Victoria & aged 4, a lively intelligent child, with big melancholy eyes....

Sarah seemed happy, both with her marriage and her work. In Lagos she taught on occasion at the Female Institution and did other work for the Church Missionary Society. She had, over the next few years, two more children, Arthur and Stella. Arthur, like Victoria, was educated in England and Europe.

Yet Sarah's health problems always remained with her, and she eventually became too weak to teach. She developed a hacking cough that would not go away, and James Davies grew more and more concerned. Sarah was diagnosed as having consumption, the disease we now know as tuberculosis. Reluctantly, she agreed to go to Madeira for treatment.

VICTORIA DAVIES, DAUGHTER OF SARAH AND JAMES

1880

Madeira— The Final Days

MADEIRA is a beautiful island off the coast of Portugal. Along the climbing slopes, neat, red-tiled houses with stark white walls formed crisp patterns that caught the eyes of the ship passengers headed for Funchal, the island's largest city. The waters around Madeira in 1880 were always clear and refreshing, the reflected clouds were always peaceful. The temperature rarely varied and the air was remarkably pure and dry.

During the winter, the snow falling high in the mountains scarcely affected the temperature at ground level. In the spring, the melted snows cascaded down the mountainsides in sparkling streams of clear water. Noted primarily for its wine industry and always bustling with tourists, Madeira was also known as a place where people with lung problems could recover.

As a child, the African princess that people came to

know as Sarah Forbes Bonetta, or "Sally," had survived the massacre of her people in the raid at Okeadan. Miraculously, she had escaped being sacrificed in the court of King Gezo of Dahomey. She had every reason to believe she would recover to return to her family and the work she had chosen for herself in Africa.

Outside the Royal Edinburgh Hotel where she stayed, Sarah could see rows of neatly landscaped jacaranda trees. The crisp morning air would find gardeners hand watering the hotel's lawns. The beauty of the place buoyed her spirits as she wrote to Mama Schoen.

ROYAL EDINBURGH HOTEL

FUNCHAL, MADEIRA

APRIL 7, 1880

My dear Mama Schoen,

I received a letter from you at Lagos the Sunday, as I started for this Island the next Tuesday, & since being here so ill as I was have been obliged to keep quiet; writing which I always liked has become also a task. I nearly died in Lagos this last illness

I had in January, & the cough I told you of, seeming rather to increase than otherwise. My poor husband who has had enough trouble to kill two ordinary men, made up his mind at the instigation of the doctor to send me here for some months change & here I am with Stella & her nurse for an indefinite period. The day after tomorrow makes one month since our arrival. I am slowly picking up strength, but the cold winds, which even here is to be felt sometimes, do not improve the cough, still it is much better to what it was in Lagos. The doctor says he will cure me in six months, & you must know, that my lungs are affected besides my throat being sore from the irritation of coughing.

Stella keeps well & seems quite to like Madeira. Is not that fortunate? I think it agrees with her. I have not seen much of the place, as the doctor forbids my walking far or even much driving. There are beautiful mountains all around us & lovely flowers, such excursions one could make here climbing over the mountains to the other side. There are two or three nice family parties in this hotel staying, they are all very pleasant. Last week Mrs. Burton from the Female Institution or as it is now termed the "Annie Walsh Memorial School" arrived on two months sick leave. I never knew her before only her sister who died at Lagos, Mrs. Faulkner. I heard from Victoria, it seems she is in England; the climate of that part of France she was at not agreeing with her; whether she will return there or not is uncertain, but she would not return to that school in any case I fancy. Meanwhile she will keep quiet and regain her strength at Mrs. Christie's and will be studying at home quietly till her father decides what is to be done. I should like her to perfect the languages German & French & her music. It is only in the two countries one can accomplish this, I know. We have nothing to give her, but a good education which will always make her independent.

Sarah seemed to feel stronger and had set a goal for herself — to be cured in six months. But four months after her letter from Madeira, we find this entry in Queen Victoria's diary.

After luncheon...saw poor Victoria Davies, my black godchild, now 17, who heard this morning of the death of her dear mother at Madeira. The poor child was dreadfully upset & distressed, & only got the news as she was starting to come here, so that she could not put off coming. Her father has failed in business, which aggravated her poor mother's illness. A young brother & a little sister, only 5, were with their mother. Victoria seems a nice girl, very black & with very pronounced negro features. I shall give her an annuity....

Sarah had once requested that when she died she be buried at sea as Commander Forbes had been. That wish never came to be. She was, instead, buried in Funchal, Madeira, in August 1880.

Sarah's children were educated in Europe. Victoria

would visit her godmother, Queen Victoria, throughout her life. The Queen would live until 1901, and Victoria Davies would be one of her last visitors.

EPILOGUE

THERE ARE many things to wonder about Sarah. The estimate by Queen Victoria put her birth in 1843, which means she lived less than thirty-eight years. During those years there were times of grave danger, of high adventure, of soaring triumphs, and crushing tragedies. There are also many questions concerning Sarah's life to which I could not find answers. Had she, as Commander Forbes once suggested, simply erased the memory of her first years from her mind? Did she not remember her African name?

What were her dreams for her own future when she lived with the Schoens? What images came to her as she rode in the pony cart with the royal children? How often did she think of Dahomey? Of King Gezo?

Sarah spent a lifetime in loss. She lost her parents, her tribe, her entire village to the Dahomans involved in the slave trade. Later she would lose Commander Forbes, her adoptive father, her home with the Schoens, even England, her adopted country. Still her last letter, written when she was desperately ill, held a message of hope.

It is difficult to sum up her life. She was both unfortunate in her losses, and fortunate that those losses were not greater. She lost so many chances for fulfillment, and yet received so many different opportunities. She seemed to find a measure of comfort wherever she was, but was destined to be apart from the world in which she lived. Throughout all of her turmoil and triumphs, she was always forgiving in her outlook, and gracious in her manner. She remained, always, a princess.

SELECTED BIBLIOGRAPHY

BOOKS

Forbes, Frederick E. *Dahomey and the Dahomans.* London: Longman, Brown, Green and Longmans, 1851.

Longford, Elizabeth. *Queen Victoria: Born to Succeed.* New York: Harper and Row, 1964.

Mayhew, Henry. *London Labour and the London Poor.* London: Griffin, Bohn, and Company, 1861–1862.

Newbery, C.W. *British Policy towards West Africa: Select Documents 1786-1874.* London: Oxford University Press, 1965.

Pool, Daniel. *What Jane Austin Ate and Charles Dickens Knew.* New York: Touchstone, 1993.

Schoen, J.F. and Crowther, S.A. *Journal of an Expedition up the Niger in 1841.* London: Frank Cass and Company, 1843.

Stock, Eugene. *History of the Church Missionary Society.* London: Church Missionary Society, 1899.

Walvin, James. *The Black Presence: A Documentary History of the Negro in England, 1555–1860.* London: Orbach and Chambers, Ltd., 1971.

NEWSPAPERS

Anti-Slavery Reporter, 3rd series, X (1862), 194 and XII (1864), 268. London: British and Foreign Anti-Slavery Society.

Brittania, November 1850.

The Church Missionary Gleaner, June 1887.

The Illustrated London News, various from 1845 to 1875.

London Times, various.

Acknowledgments and Credits

Many people were helpful in tracking down clues to Sarah's life. Among the most helpful were, in England, Rosemary Keen, researcher, and Frances Dimond, Curator of the Royal Photographic Collection. Thanks, too, to the librarians at the Newspaper Archives at Colindale, the Gillingham Public Library, the Church Mission Society archives, and the Brighton Public Library, and to the staff of the Family Record Office in London.

In the United States Eileen Weiss helped in the initial assembling of the documents. It was Priya Nair who gently nudged the mountain of documents, letters, research, and images into book form.

Special thanks to Howard Daitz, who offered valuable suggestions for the photographic research, and also to Charles Cogan at Northwestern University for fact-checking the manuscript.

CREDITS

Pages ii, 4, 11, 12: From *Dahomey and the Dahomans* by Frederick E. Forbes; Longman, Brown, Green and Longmans, 1851

Page xiv: Map by Laszlo Kubinyi

Pages 16, 122: Reprinted by permission of the Syndics of Cambridge University Library

Pages 22, 113: From the author's collection; photograph by John J. Mayall

Page 26: From the author's collection; photograph by C. Silvis

Pages 29, 85: Courtesy of *The Illustrated London News* Picture Library

Page 32: From the author's collection; photograph by Strohmeyer & Wyman

Pages 34, 35: From the author's collection; photograph by George Washington Wilson

Pages 37, 76, 129: The Royal Archives © 1998 Her Majesty Queen Elizabeth II

Page 42: From the collection of the New-York Historical Society

Pages 49, 103, 105, 109, 118, 120, 132: From the author's collection

Page 50: Reprinted with permission of the United Methodist Church Archives, Madison, New Jersey

Pages 54, 70: Reprinted with permission of the Church Mission Society Archive

Page 75: Reprinted with permission of Corbis-Bettman; woodcut by Gustav Doré

Page 100: From the author's collection; photograph by Alexander Bassano

Page 115: Reprinted with permission of the National Gallery of Canada, Ottawa

Page 121: Reproduced with permission of the County Archivist, copyright reserved

Page 141: From the author's collection; monogram appeared on Sarah Forbes Bonetta's personal stationery

Excerpts from Queen Victoria's diary pages 24, 30, 72, 128, 136; Letter from Reverend Schmid to Charles Phipps pages 44-45; List of articles purchased for Sarah page 58: Reprinted with the gracious permission of Her Majesty Queen Elizabeth II

Endpapers: From the author's collection; a portion of this letter, written by Sarah Forbes Bonetta, is transcribed on pages 91-92